THE TWELVE DAYS OF CHRISTMAS

THE
MILLBROOK
PRESS

BROOKFIELD,
CONNECTICUT

THE TWELVE DAYS OF CHRISTMAS

ILLUSTRATED BY
BRIAN WILDSMITH

The first day of Christmas,
My true love sent to me
A partridge in a pear tree.

The second day of Christmas,
My true love sent to me
Two turtle doves, and
A partridge in a pear tree.

The third day of Christmas,
My true love sent to me
Three French hens,
Two turtle doves, and
A partridge in a pear tree.

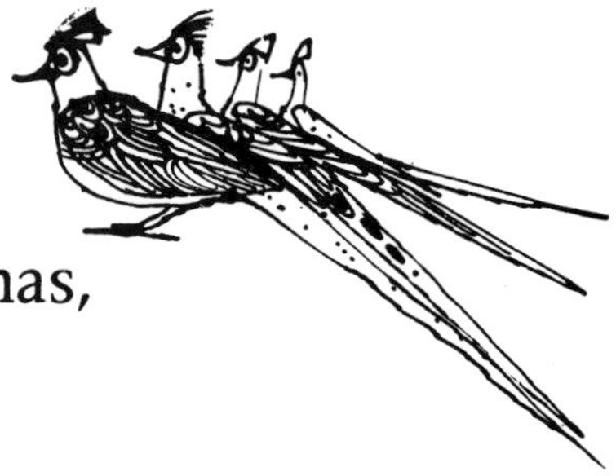

The fourth day of Christmas,
My true love sent to me
Four colly birds,
Three French hens,
Two turtle doves, and
A partridge in a pear tree.

The fifth day of Christmas,
My true love sent to me
Five gold rings,
Four colly birds,
Three French hens,
Two turtle doves, and
A partridge in a pear tree.

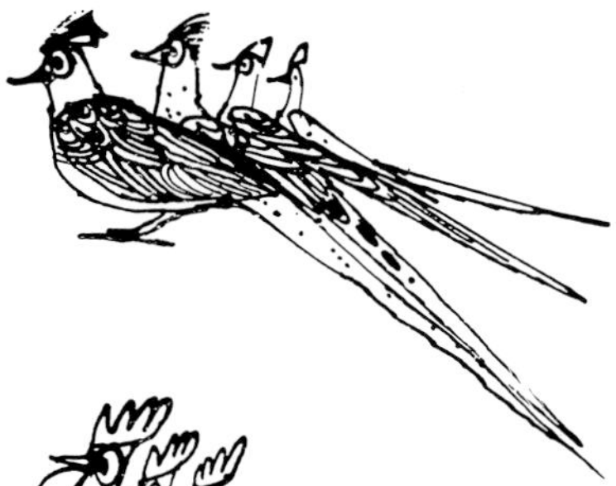

The sixth day of Christmas,
My true love sent to me
Six geese a-laying,
Five gold rings,
Four colly birds,
Three French hens,
Two turtle doves, and
A partridge in a pear tree.

The seventh day of Christmas,
My true love sent to me
Seven swans a-swimming,
Six geese a-laying,
Five gold rings,
Four colly birds,
Three French hens,
Two turtle doves, and
A partridge in a pear tree.

The eighth day of Christmas,
My true love sent to me
Eight maids a-milking,
Seven swans a-swimming,
Six geese a-laying,
Five gold rings,
Four colly birds,
Three French hens,
Two turtle doves, and
A partridge in a pear tree.

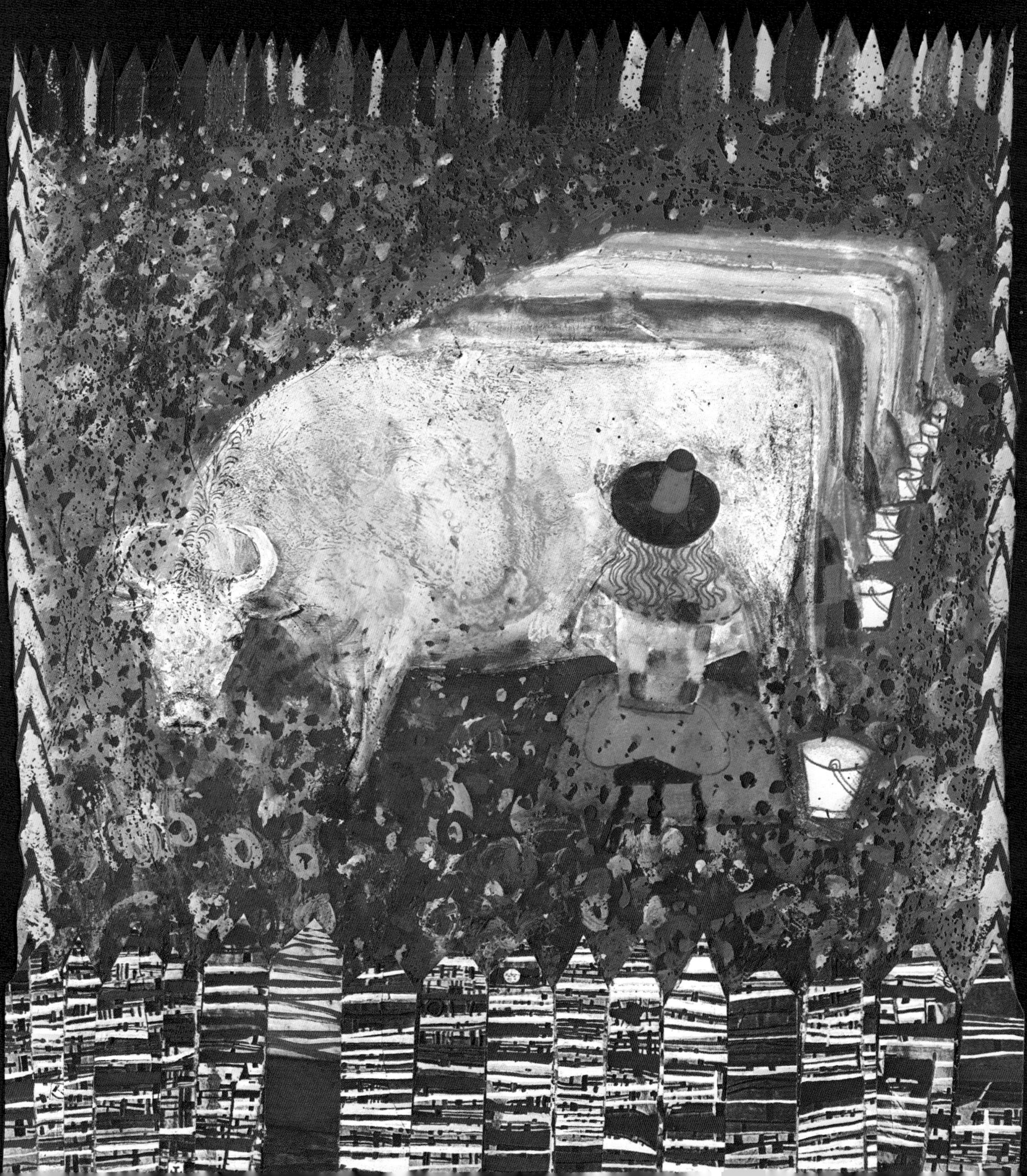

The ninth day of Christmas,
My true love sent to me
Nine drummers drumming,
Eight maids a-milking,
Seven swans a-swimming,
Six geese a-laying,
Five gold rings,
Four colly birds,
Three French hens,
Two turtle doves, and
A partridge in a pear tree.

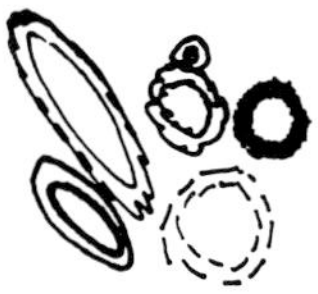
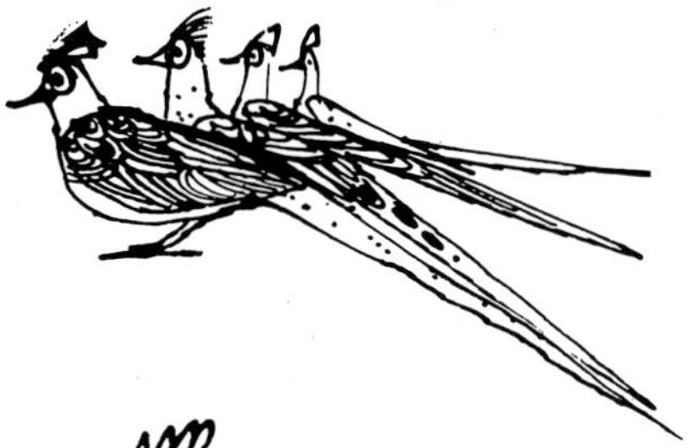

The tenth day of Christmas,
My true love sent to me
Ten pipers piping,
Nine drummers drumming,
Eight maids a-milking,
Seven swans a-swimming,
Six geese a-laying,
Five gold rings,
Four colly birds,
Three French hens,
Two turtle doves, and
A partridge in a pear tree.

The eleventh day of Christmas,
My true love sent to me
Eleven ladies dancing,
Ten pipers piping,
Nine drummers drumming,
Eight maids a-milking,
Seven swans a-swimming,
Six geese a-laying,
Five gold rings,
Four colly birds,
Three French hens,
Two turtle doves, and
A partridge in a pear tree.

The twelfth day of Christmas,
My true love sent to me
Twelve lords a-leaping,
Eleven ladies dancing,
Ten pipers piping,
Nine drummers drumming,
Eight maids a-milking,
Seven swans a-swimming,
Six geese a-laying,
Five gold rings,
Four colly birds,
Three French hens,
Two turtle doves, and
A partridge in a pear tree.

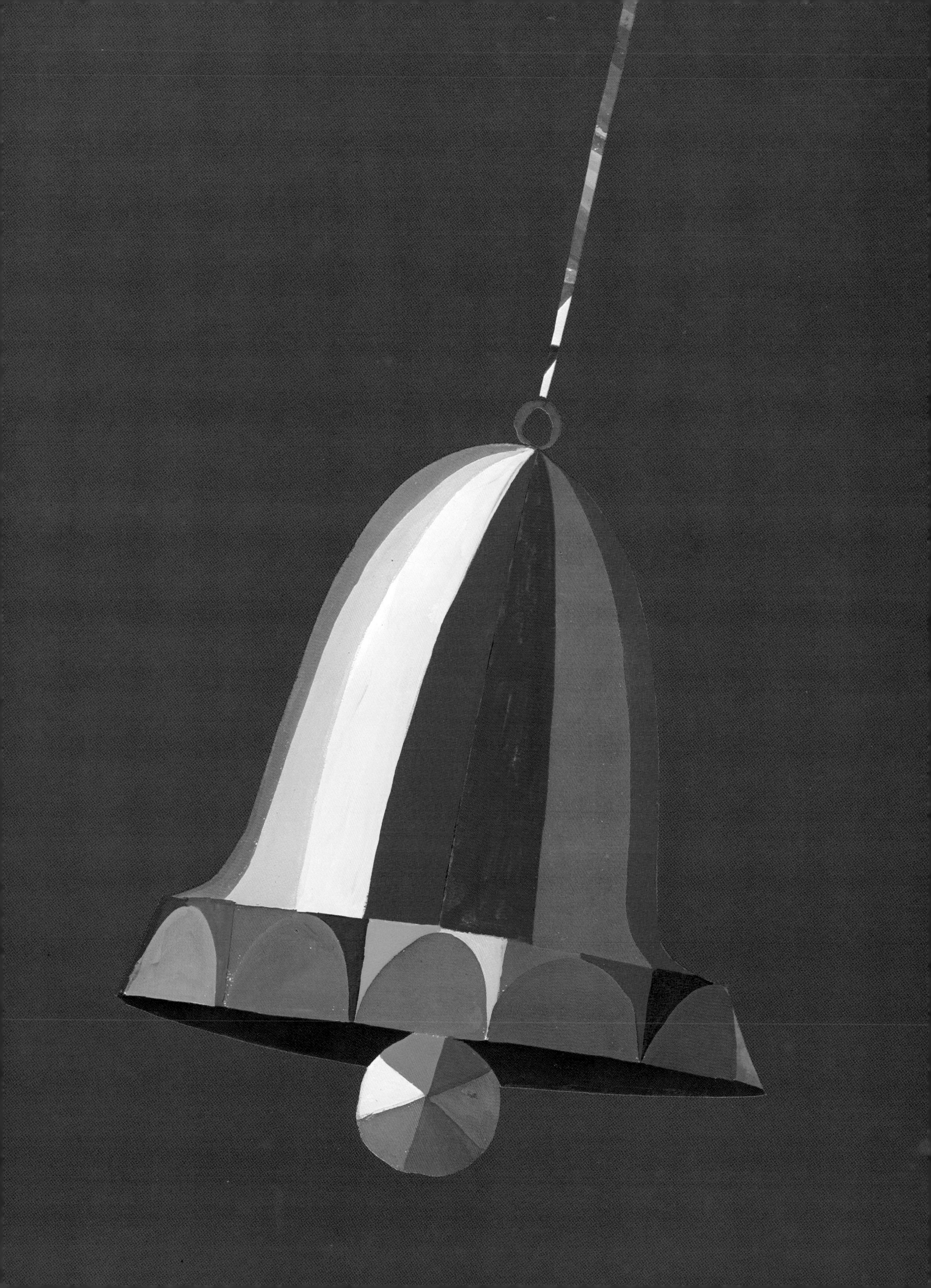

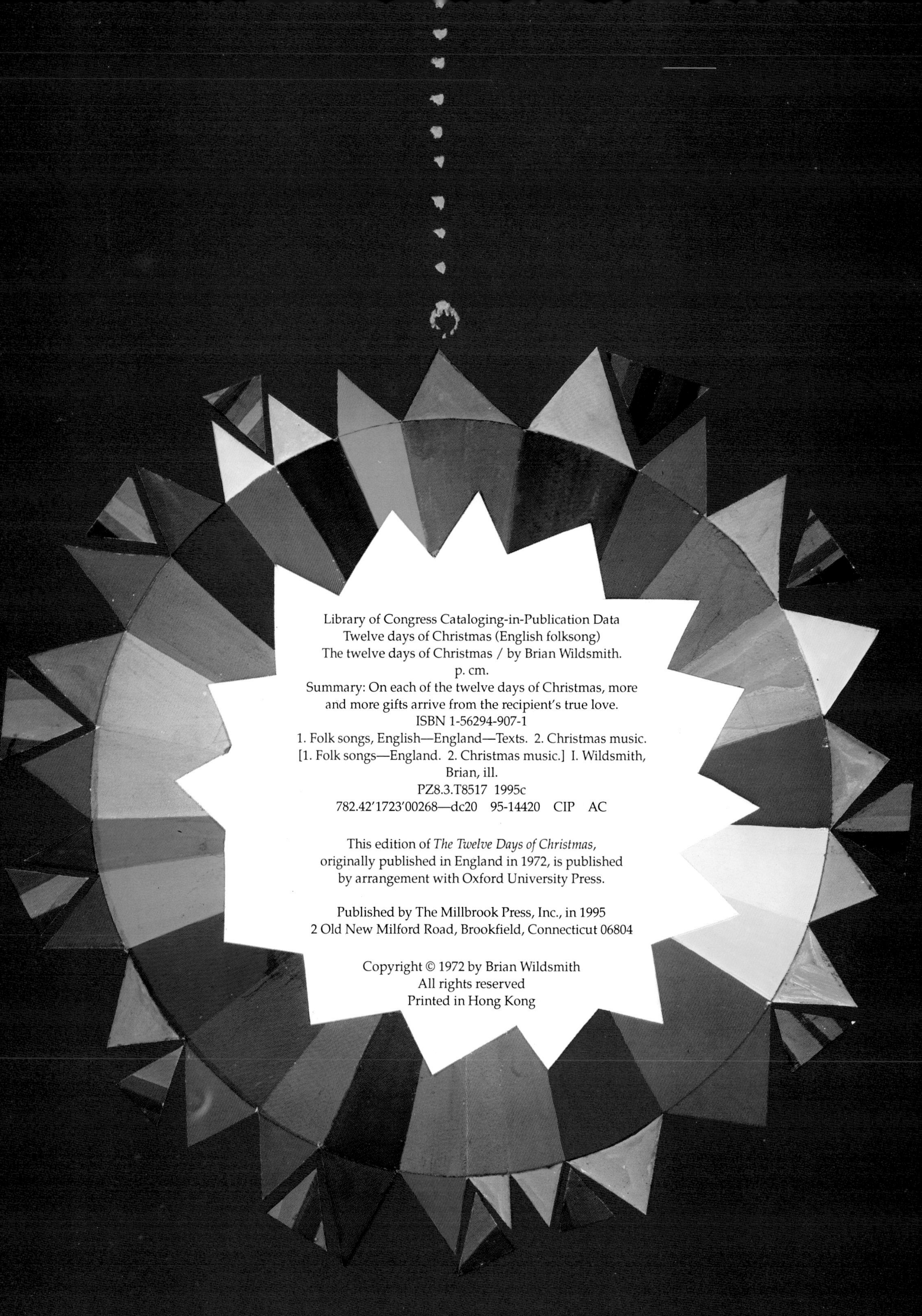

Library of Congress Cataloging-in-Publication Data
Twelve days of Christmas (English folksong)
The twelve days of Christmas / by Brian Wildsmith.
p. cm.
Summary: On each of the twelve days of Christmas, more and more gifts arrive from the recipient's true love.
ISBN 1-56294-907-1
1. Folk songs, English—England—Texts. 2. Christmas music. [1. Folk songs—England. 2. Christmas music.] I. Wildsmith, Brian, ill.
PZ8.3.T8517 1995c
782.42'1723'00268—dc20 95-14420 CIP AC

This edition of *The Twelve Days of Christmas*, originally published in England in 1972, is published by arrangement with Oxford University Press.

Published by The Millbrook Press, Inc., in 1995
2 Old New Milford Road, Brookfield, Connecticut 06804